Little
Champ

To my three most favorite people in the whole world!

I hope you enjoy reading this book, as it is about one of my favorite places to be, the other favorite place for me is with you!

Love,
Granny

♡ ♡ ♡

Little Champ

Written and illustrated by

JIM ARNOSKY

Onion River Press

Underhill, Vermont

To Bob, Loretta, and Troy

The author wishes to acknowledge Joseph W. Zarzynski
for his years of research into Lake Champlain's mysterious phenomenon
known simply as "Champ," and for his wonderfully informative book
on the subject, *Champ: Beyond the Legend*.

Onion River Press, 23 Wildberry Lane, Underhill, Vermont 05489
Printed in the United States of America
Hardcover published by G.P. Putnam's Sons in 1995.
Paperback published by Onion River Press in 2001.
Text set in Palatino.

Library of Congress Cataloging-in-Publication Data
Arnosky, Jim.
  Little Champ / written and illustrated by Jim Arnosky.
    p. cm.
  Summary: Bobby and Gina visit their grandparents on Lake Champlain and learn about
the legendary monster that supposedly inhabits the lake.
  ISBN 0-9657144-5-4
  [1. Champlain, Lake--Fiction.   2. Monsters--Fiction.   3. Brothers and sisters--Fiction.   4.
Grandparents--Fiction.   5. Vermont--Fiction.]   I. Title.

PZ7.A7384 Li 2001
[Fic]--dc21   2001024659

This is not a true story,
but I wish it were.

JIM ARNOSKY
CRINKLE COVE, 1994

Chapter 1

It was the first day of spring, but Gina was cold and shivering as she stood on the shore of the island looking out over Lake Champlain.

"Bobby, do you think the ice will ever melt?"

"Sure it will, Gina. But I don't know when."

Bobby and Gina always spent part of the summer here in Vermont at their grandparents' home, but this year they had come early because the family was moving to California.

"What do you think Mom and Dad are doing right now?"

"How would I know? They're probably packing up the furniture and stuff for the moving van," Bobby answered.

"Do you think it will be cold like this in California?" Gina asked.

"Not where we're going to live! Dad says the beach is only fifteen minutes from our new house."

"Oh, well, when summer gets here we'll have some fun. Grandma wants me to help out in the store," Gina told Bobby.

"Grandpa's going to let me pump gas at the marina. I can't wait!" Bobby said.

Gina looked out across the lake. Broad patches of ice floated on the surface. A gull landed on an ice floe and, as the bird touched down, the ice crumbled and sank. The gull simply flapped back up in the air and flew on.

"Bobby!" Gina shouted. "The ice is soft! It must be melting!"

Bobby paid no attention. He was searching for something on the shore. "What are you looking for?" Gina asked.

"A zebra stone." He picked up a small dark stone, examined it, and then dropped it back on the ground.

Zebra stones are black rocks with lines of white quartz running through them. Their grandfather had a few for sale in the store.

Gina began looking for zebra stones with her brother. "Bobby, do you think you'll like California?"

"I don't know. I hope so."

"What's California like, anyway?"

Bobby raised his voice. "I don't know! And stop asking me about everything! You've been asking me questions about California ever since we got here."

2

Gina threw down the stone she was holding. "You don't have to be so mean!"

Just then Bobby spotted a large zebra stone and ran to pick it up. "Look, Gina. Look at this beauty!" It was smooth and round and black, with a zigzagged vein of sparkling white quartz. "I'm going to sell it in Grandpa's store!"

"No," Gina said. "Throw it in the lake as far as you can. It'll be for us, for good luck."

Bobby liked the idea. He went into his best big-league windup and pitched the rock as hard as he could. The zebra stone sailed high in the air, then plummeted down, plunging out of sight through a patch of soft ice.

The stone sank slowly, rotating like a tiny black-and-white planet in the icy water, before coming to rest on a gravelly shoal. A trio of perch circled to inspect the new object. Suddenly the perch dashed away, frightened by a dark, shadowy figure moving over the shoal.

Midway between the undersurface of the ice and the lake bottom, a gigantic animal was swimming. It had a long neck and a massive torso. The creature paddled itself along with four large flippers—two front and two back. A short, powerful tail waving steadily from side to side kept the enormous body stable in the water.

Another animal, similar in shape but much smaller, swam over the gravel. It was young, more swift and agile than its mother. The youngster somersaulted in the water, then swam a quick circle around its mother's tail. Spotting the black-and-white stone on the gravel shoal, it swam down and, using its snout, began playfully pushing the rock along.

The creature's head was small, its eyes large. It had a broad reptilian grin fixed on its face, and when it opened its mouth to bite at the quartz in the stone, rows of white pointed teeth shined in the cool blue light. Two large nostrils situated high on its snout released small streams of tiny bubbles into the water.

Abruptly, the young creature abandoned the zebra stone and swam up to breathe a large bubble of air trapped under the ice, then dived back down. Forgetting all about the black-and-white stone, it started grubbing with its snout in the pebbly bottom. A cloud of silt rose in the water, and out of it, a crayfish darted. The youngster snapped the crayfish up in its mouth and gobbled it down.

The mother swam over her offspring, arching her broad back until it rubbed up against the frozen undersurface of the lake. The force of her motion pushed the whole ice floe up a few inches, and the frozen surface in flux made a loud moaning sound.

♦ ♦ ♦

Back on shore Gina and Bobby heard the eerie noise.

"Listen to that!" Bobby said. "It's the ice moving in the lake. Grandpa says it makes loud noises when it's melting and breaking up."

They stood still and quiet, looking out at the icy lake, waiting for another moaning sound. A gull flew overhead. Its piercing call ended their ice-watching mood.

"C'mon," Bobby said, "let's go back to the store."

Gina dashed ahead, laughing. "Last one home is an old zebra stone!"

Chapter 2

Gennard's General Store stood in the center of the busy little lakeshore village. The children's grand-mother was standing on a small ladder, replacing a shelf's stock of flannel shirts with colorful summer T-shirts. At the register their grandfather was ringing up a purchase while his customer leafed through a book that was on display. Gina and Bobby came running in.

"What do you think about this Lake Champlain monster?" the customer casually asked. The book was about the lake's legendary monster.

"Loch Ness has Nessie; we have Champ!" Grandpa told the woman. "Most people around the lake rarely speak of Champ, but a good many of them believe it exists. Either they've seen it for themselves or know someone who has."

Picking up her bag of groceries, the woman asked, "Have you ever seen it?" Grandpa said, "No, but I sure would like to." He leaned toward the woman.

"You know, whenever there is a recent sighting, it gets very little serious publicity. But the people who swear they've seen it—they're dead serious! It's no joke to them."

The customer was enthralled. She rested her groceries back down on the counter. A young couple who had been browsing in the store overheard the talk of Champ, and they came over to hear more. Bobby went to the counter to listen. Gina listened with her grandmother. Grandpa was on center stage. His eyes brightened. His cheeks flushed.

He told of the lake's legendary monster—about the horned serpent of Indian lore, and of famed explorer Samuel de Champlain's supposedly seeing the creature.

The listeners hung on every word as Grandpa told of unidentified animals seen in the lake over the years. "Eyewitness descriptions vary," Grandpa continued. "Some people see only a dark serpentine shape wriggling through the water. Others report seeing a series of undulating humps. I've read accounts that describe only one great humped back rising up out of the water, then slowly sinking back down."

Grandpa lowered his voice to draw his listeners closer. "Then there are the most curious sightings—of a snakelike head on a long tapering neck sticking up out of the water."

Suddenly Grandpa spotted his neighbor Fred Sinclair and Fred's son Freddy coming into the store. Abruptly he changed his tone from that of mystery and wonder to something approaching skepticism. "Of course," he said, "we do have sturgeon almost as long as a boat in the lake. Could be that's what people are seeing. Just lake sturgeon wallowing in shallow water."

When it came to Champ, Fred Sinclair was a confirmed skeptic. He mocked those who claimed to have seen Champ. And knowing of his neighbor's enthusiasm for the subject, he especially enjoyed jibing Grandpa. He stepped between the people gathered around the counter and laughed. "You rambling on about Champ again, Charlie?" Mr. Sinclair faced the others and said, "Take it from me, folks, there ain't no such thing! In all my years fishing on the lake, I've never seen anything remotely resembling a monster."

Grandpa leaned over the counter. "What about all those who say they have? What about Clyde and his son Chad? They saw it together. They were fishing near the jetty. The thing churned up the water just ten feet away from the bow of the boat."

Mr. Sinclair looked Grandpa in the eye. "Chad sits up front in that skiff, right in his dad's way. He probably saw something big in the water, a big old musky swirling or splashing after a perch." Then he

added jokingly, "You sound convinced, Charlie. You seen it, have ya?"

Grandpa was miffed. "You know I haven't. But I'd like to see what it is all these folks are seeing."

Fred Sinclair threw up his arms. "Well, I sure haven't seen it. And I don't believe any such thing exists!"

Grandpa winked at Bobby and Gina. Then he turned to Mr. Sinclair. "What if you did see it, Fred? What if you were out there some morning guiding one of your city slickers to a hot spot for pike, and instead of a fish rising to your bait, a big long-necked beast rose up . . ."

Freddy's eyes widened. The customers around the counter all watched as Grandpa raised his arm high over his head, mimicking a monster's long neck. Suddenly he snapped his hand toward Fred Sinclair. Everyone flinched at the motion. "What then?" Grandpa asked mischievously. "Would you be seeing things too?"

The customers were entranced. Even Mr. Sinclair was captivated by Grandpa's talk. But he snapped out of it and joked loudly, "I'd probably have been drinking too much of that sour apple cider you sell. Come on, Freddy. Let's go home before we start believing in lake monsters like old Charlie!"

Everyone returned to their business. Customers left

carrying their purchases. More customers came in. Grandpa whistled as he worked behind the counter. Grandma and Gina laughed as they straightened up the shelf full of T-shirts. For the time being, the legend of Champ was laid to rest.

That evening Bobby and Gina sat at the dining-room table doing their homework. When Gina finished, she began to draw a picture of her grandfather, who was sitting and reading the newspaper. Bobby watched as his sister sketched. He liked watching her draw. She was so good at it. When Gina was done, she took the portrait over to her grandmother, who held it up to show her husband.

"Is my nose that big?" he asked. Then, holding his palm to his face, he said, "Well, I guess it is!" Everybody laughed.

"Draw Champ!" Bobby suggested to Gina. Gina drew a few lines, then stopped. "What does Champ's face look like, Grandpa?" she asked.

Grandpa thought for a second, then said, "Well, Gina, it's hard to say. Some folks say Champ has a horse's head. Others say he has a face like a boa constrictor."

Grandma added, "I've heard people say Champ looks like a giant seal, with big brown eyes and flippers."

Grandpa held his arms out and paddled in the air with them as if they were flippers. He puffed up his cheeks and crossed his eyes. Bobby and Gina laughed.

Grandma enjoyed seeing her husband playing.

"What about the horns?" Bobby said, holding his fingers up on his forehead. "I'm Champ and I EAT little kids!" He growled.

From all the different descriptions, Gina drew a picture of a monster—half snake, half seal—with a horse's head. She added two horns to the head and a flowing mane. Bobby watched closely. "Give it fangs!" he said. Gina added two long fangs.

Grandma glanced at the living-room clock. "Okay, kids, time to get to bed. You have school tomorrow. "

Grandma hung Gina's drawings in the kitchen on the refrigerator door. Grandpa went back to his chair and the newspaper. Bobby and Gina gathered up their homework and went upstairs to bed.

After Grandma had said good night, Gina lay in bed with the covers pulled up warmly all around her face. "Bobby," she said softly, "do you believe in Champ?"

Bobby twisted himself around under his covers to face his sister's bed. "If Grandpa thinks that Champ is real, so do I."

"Me too," Gina whispered.

"When's summer going to come? It's so cold out."

"Grandpa says soon." Bobby yawned and rolled onto his side.

But Gina was not sleepy yet. Too many images flashed through her mind—of summer on the lake, the busy store, her drawing of Champ, school, her parents, and moving to a new place, another new school, making new friends. "Bobby?" she called softly.

"Go to sleep, Gina," Bobby murmured.

"Good night, Bobby."

"'Night," Bobby mumbled back. Gina listened until she heard her brother sleeping. Then she closed her eyes. Soon she too was fast asleep.

14

Chapter 3

Every day was more like spring. The lake ice melted. Green leaves sprouted on the trees along the shore. Docks were moved out of winter storage and installed on the waterfront. Boats were launched. Every afternoon felt warmer than the day before.

By the first of June, summer weather had arrived. On the last day of school, Bobby and Gina walked home rather than taking the bus. It was a sunny, windless day. The lake, always in view on the narrow island, was sparkling blue and calm. Bobby and Gina followed the lakeshore to the jetty of rocks within sight of their grandparents' marina and store. The jetty cradled a small, deepwater cove. Bobby plopped his backpack down, and, noticing a small chunk of white quartz amid the jetty stones, picked it up and began searching for another. Gina joined in.

Out in the center of the cove, a gull floated buoyantly on the water. Suddenly the water beneath the gull bulged. The startled bird squawked and flew just as a large dark hump surfaced.

Underwater, Little Champ swam beneath his mother as she cruised through a school of perch. She lunged her long neck forward and plucked one fish out of the crowd. Then she hung suspended in the water as she swallowed it down. Little Champ caught up with the fleeing fish. One perch panicked and darted from the school. Little Champ chased it upward through the slanting rays of sunlight and splashed after the fish, snatching it just as it began to leap out into the air.

Bobby saw the commotion. He called to Gina, "Look, an otter."

Gina looked but saw only a swirl. Then the swirl became a swell as Little Champ raised his long neck up out of the water. It was no otter. Bobby and Gina knew they were seeing something strange and wonderful. Gina pressed against her brother's side, but she wasn't frightened. "It's a dinosaur!" she whispered.

"Oh my gosh!" her brother said in a hushed voice. "It's Champ!"

Bobby and Gina watched as the creature in the cove turned its head and looked in their direction. Little Champ had the perch clamped sideways in his mouth. He looked funny, not scary, and Gina giggled.

Little Champ began to tip and jerk his head, manipulating his jaws to turn the fish around so he could swallow it headfirst.

Bobby leaned toward his sister. "Just like a heron," he said.

Suddenly the water behind Little Champ bulged and swirled as his mother surfaced. Her swan-like neck movements were graceful and nonthreatening. It was a scene right out of a dinosaur book, only it was happening for real as Bobby and Gina looked on. The children watched unblinking, hardly believing what they were seeing. They looked at each other, and in that instant, both creatures submerged and disappeared. Gina and Bobby grabbed their backpacks and ran home to tell their grandparents.

Grandpa and Grandma were in the store carefully fitting together a new product display when their grandchildren came bursting in, yelling, "We saw Champ! We saw it! Down by the jetty! We saw Champ!"

"Wait a minute," Grandpa said. "Slow down. You mean you THINK you saw Champ. A lot of people see things they think are Champ—a log floating in the lake, for instance. Sometimes an odd-shaped piece of sunken driftwood suddenly buoys up to the surface and pops up out of the water."

Bobby and Gina listened. Then Gina said, "But, Grandpa, if it was a log, it was a log eating a fish."

Bobby added, "Yeah! We watched it eat a perch. It flipped the fish around to swallow it headfirst—just like a heron, only it wasn't a heron . . . it was much bigger . . . and that's not all . . ."

But before he could say any more, his grandfather said, "Hold it!" He ran to get a piece of paper and a pencil. Then he pulled a stool up to the counter and motioned to Gina to sit. "Here, Gina. Draw us a picture of exactly what you and Bobby saw."

Gina climbed up onto the stool, pulled the sheet of paper close to her, and drew a humped back and long neck. Bobby helped her by suggesting details he remembered. "Make the eyes big and dark. Give it lots of pointy teeth. It had some kind of bumps on the head. Add bumps, Gina!"

Gina added all of Bobby's suggestions plus details she remembered. She drew water rolling off the animal's back and more water dripping from its chin. She added the fish clamped sideways in the creature's mouth. As soon as she finished one figure, Gina began drawing another, larger figure. "And its momma was swimming around it," she said matter-of-factly, sketching the lines for the mother's long neck.

Their grandma stepped back in amazement. "You

were watching two? . . . A baby and its mother?" she asked.

Grandpa leaned forward. "Weren't you afraid?" he asked.

"No," Gina and Bobby answered calmly.

Then Gina explained, "It wasn't scary at all, Grandpa. It was . . . it was . . . " As she searched her mind for the word, her brother offered his own. "Real!" he said, and Gina added, "And beautiful."

"Let's all go to the jetty and have a look." He took his binoculars down from a shelf and led everyone out the door and down to the jetty.

They scanned the cove with their naked eyes as well as through the binoculars. They saw gulls, cormorants, and ducks swimming on the cove, but no Champ.

"I guess they're gone," Grandpa said. "But they can't be too far off. Tomorrow we'll launch the boat and take a look around the lake."

Bobby snapped, "ALL RIGHT!"

Gina shouted, "Yippie! We're going on a boat ride!"

On the way back home, Gina and Bobby ran ahead while their grandparents walked, enjoying the sunny afternoon. They made plans to close the store and spend the next day on *Crayfish*, Grandpa's boat.

Chapter 4

The next morning was sunny and bright. Bobby woke up earlier than usual, eager to help launch the boat. By the time Gina was awake and dressed, *Crayfish* was floating in its slip and almost ready to go.

Bobby watched his grandfather carefully inspect each gas tank and fuel line for leaks. Grandpa hummed as he worked. *Crayfish* had everything Bobby thought a boat should have—a pilot house, a nautical steering wheel, a ship-to-shore radio, a horn, and a white life ring with CRAYFISH painted on it.

"Grandpa, why did you name your boat Crayfish?" Bobby asked.

"Well, Bobby, this boat was built for the sea, for lobster fishing along the New England coast. When I brought it here to the freshwater of Lake Champlain, Grandma suggested I name the boat after our own little freshwater lobsters—crayfish."

Grandpa gently closed the engine compartment hatch. "Now she's ready, and here comes the rest of the crew!"

Gina and her grandmother were headed toward *Crayfish*, loaded down with supplies—lunch, binoculars, Grandma's 35mm camera, and four flotation cushions. Grandpa took the lunch basket from Gina, and Bobby offered a hand to Grandma as she stepped from the dock down onto *Crayfish*'s deck. They loaded the supplies and stowed them in the cabin. Then Grandpa started up the engine and called for his crew to cast off the dock lines. Slowly *Crayfish* putt-putt-putted away from the dock, between the moored sailboats, out of the marina, and through the marked channel that led to the open water of the lake.

"Champ, here we come!" Grandpa called out over the lake.

Gina and Bobby stood on the deck and watched their grandfather steer. He reached forward on the console and pushed a tiny red button. *"TOOT-TOOT!"* went *Crayfish*'s horn.

"Neat!" Gina shouted.

"Cool!" Bobby agreed.

Grandpa steered around the last channel marker and cruised into the deep, broad lake. Grandma sat back in a deck chair near the stern, enjoying the air and the water.

Bobby and Gina stood near the helm. One at a time Grandpa let them take the wheel. Gina had to stand on the ice chest to see over the console, but she

steered the boat just as well as Bobby. Then Grandpa took the helm again.

After about five minutes, Grandpa called out, "There's the jetty!" He turned the wheel a hard left to maneuver safely around the rocky point. Then, throttling down, he eased the wheel back to the right and headed directly into the cove.

The cove looked different from the boat. It took a little while for Bobby to pick out the place where he and Gina had seen the creatures rise out of the water. Then suddenly he realized *Crayfish* was floating right over the spot. He pointed to the water near the boat. "That's where Little Champ was eating the perch."

All four looked down into the water. It was murky and dark. Grandpa checked the chart. "It's forty feet deep right here," he said. "And a little ways out, it drops to fifty. Maybe those two were feeding along the drop-off the way big fish do."

Gina had always thought the lake had a flat bottom, like a giant swimming pool. Bobby did too. Now they both leaned over the rail and peered down into the depths, each trying to imagine the steep submerged drop-off their grandfather had just described. The idea of there being an underwater world of cliffs and valleys was new and exciting.

Just then Bobby spotted something across the cove, floating on the surface. It was round and shiny and it was moving. Grandpa looked through his binoculars. He couldn't exactly tell what the thing was, but it was moving slowly toward them.

The whole crew watched as the thing came closer and closer, sometimes surfacing, sometimes dipping under. Once, they saw what appeared to be a humped back rising up. But the closer it came, the smaller it looked.

"It's a turtle!" Grandma said.

"Wow! That's a really old snapper! Look at the size of that monster! Its shell must be nearly two feet across!" Grandpa cried.

Bobby and Gina were disappointed it wasn't Champ, but they had never seen such a big turtle. When it finally dipped under and swam away, they both murmured, "Wow!"

Grandpa then put the idling engine in gear, turned the steering wheel, and headed *Crayfish* back out to the broad lake. They enjoyed the rest of the morning cruising slowly through waves sparkling in the sunlight. They watched scores of gulls floating and flying and saw huge schools of minnows swimming by. They didn't see anything else that even resembled Champ, but they were having so much fun that it really didn't matter. Grandpa reveled in piloting his little boat this way and that way and scribing great circles on the lake. Bobby used a notebook he found in the cabin to keep a log describing everything they'd seen. Gina drew pictures in the margins.

While setting up a luncheon on the deck, Grandma spotted a string of colorful plastic fish floats. She tied the string of floats around Gina's waist. Gina hula danced around like an exotic island girl and posed for a snapshot. "I guess I'm not going to get a picture of Champ today," Grandma said. "But I like this picture just as well. We'll send a copy to your mom and dad."

After lunch the wind picked up and the lake turned choppy. "It's time to head her in," Grandpa said. The crew agreed and they rode the white-capped waves all the way back home.

Beneath the wind and waves, the underworld of the lake remained calm—a watery realm of sprawling weed beds, rocky ledges, and gently rolling valleys. A great school of smelt threaded through blue-green vegetation, all rising in unison like a flock of small birds to surmount each ridge or pile of boulders jutting up out of the weeds. A gang of big fat bass rested suspended in the cool water above a ledge where the lake's bottom abruptly dropped a hundred feet or more to an even darker, colder depth. Through this spectacular ravine swam Champ and Little Champ.

Little Champ stayed close behind his mother, mimicking her every move. Together they swam over

lumps and bumps in the terrain and cruised into a long corridor eroded in the silt. The corridor deepened and turned toward a wall of rock. At the base of the wall was a cavernous hole. Mother Champ swam into the dark hole. Little Champ followed. He could no longer see his mother ahead, but he felt the force of her movements in the water.

Little Champ sensed that they were swimming straight at first, then turning sharply. Suddenly he felt his body shift and he knew that he was swimming upward. He paddled hard with his front flippers, using strong downward strokes to climb blindly up the vertical shaft. Up, up the two animals swam until at last they reached a plateau and the tunnel leveled off again. Like a giant flooded wormhole, the passageway twisted this way and that way. The water temperature increased. The water pressure decreased. Small pockets of air were trapped against the tunnel top. Little Champ lifted his head and breathed in some air. He heard his mother doing the same.

The tunnel widened. Each new pocket of trapped air was larger than the previous one. When there was as much air as water, the tunnel opened up to form a large chamber. It was a world of sound and smell and touch, but not of sight. There were echoing noises of other bodies moving around in the water. Familiar-sounding grunts and low whistling groans identified the other creatures in the chamber to Little Champ as adults of his own kind. Some were sleeping. Others were communicating quietly. Their vocal sounds and splashes came from every corner of the cave. Little Champ draped his neck over his mother's broad back. He closed his eyes and went to sleep.

Chapter 5

For two weeks Grandpa, Bobby, and Gina spent every morning cruising the lake, searching for Champ. Grandma stayed ashore to mind the store. Bobby wore his grandmother's camera around his neck to take pictures if they saw Champ. They saw salmon leaping after floating insects. They passed a small island crowded with nesting cormorants. They discovered a weedy backwater where beavers had built a lodge. They spotted deer along the shore. One morning they saw a raccoon swimming in the lake.

Bobby logged their adventures in his notebook and Gina drew pictures in the margins. She was finishing a drawing of *Crayfish* and everybody on board when Bobby shouted, "Look at that!"

Grandpa quickly throttled down, bringing *Crayfish* to a halt. Bobby yelled again, "There! Under the water!"

The rest soon saw what Bobby saw. It was long

and dark and appeared to be moving slowly in the water. Grandpa eased the boat in reverse to stay clear of the thing as it moved nearer to them. Bobby held the small camera ready. "It's as long as the boat!" he cried.

Gina looked through her binoculars and focused on the object underwater. "It's shaped like Champ," she said. "But it's not Champ."

"It's a log," Grandpa concluded. "An old driftwood log suspended in the water."

The next day the crew set out extra early to explore a very deep section of the lake. Grandpa had stayed up late the night before installing an electronic fish-finder, and he was eager to try it out. Freddy Sinclair's mom agreed to watch the store, so Grandma could go along, and Freddy too.

Grandpa was like a kid with a new toy. As soon as they had cleared the channel, he turned on the fish-finder and explained how the little screen would alert them if any living creature swam beneath the boat. As he spoke, a dot popped onto the screen, accompanied by a little *blip* noise. "That's a fish!" Grandpa said. A larger shape appeared and the screen went *blip* again.

"That must be a bigger fish," Bobby said.

"What will it do for Champ?" Gina asked her grandfather.

Grandpa scratched his head and answered honestly. "Well, I don't really know. It may just show a long black blur and go blip-blip-blip-blip-blip!" The sonar blipped again, and this time an arc appeared in the center of the screen.

"Now, that one is a long-bodied fish, a pike maybe," Grandpa said, pointing to the shape. He turned to the children, scrunched up his face so his teeth showed, and snarled, "A great big toothy pike!"

Freddy's eyes widened and his throat made a gulping sound. Grandma put her hand on the boy's shoulder. She sensed that he was starting to feel uneasy.

Grandpa spent the next two hours cruising slowly, fascinated by the little sonar screen as it revealed the contour of the lake bottom. Bobby and Freddy watched the screen only when it signaled fish swimming beneath the boat. At the top of a blank page in Bobby's log book, Gina made a tiny drawing of *Crayfish*. Then beneath the drawing of the boat, on the rest of the page, she drew a fish shape every time the sonar went *blip*. In a very short time she had filled the entire page with fishy shapes. "My lord," her grandmother said, "I never realized how many fish lived in the lake."

It was the middle of the afternoon when Grandpa noticed a smear forming on the screen, without any blipping sound at all. "Look at this!" he called out. The smear continued. Something large was swimming or floating in the water about eighty feet below.

"What do you make of it?" Grandpa asked Grandma.

"Could it be a school of smelt?"

"Could be," her husband said. "Smelt live in this part of the lake. A huge school might register as one long shape."

"Why no sounds?" Gina asked. "If it were fish, wouldn't it be making blipping sounds?"

Grandpa had no answer.

As soon as one smear trailed off the screen, another, smaller smear began to form, then suddenly it disappeared. Grandpa made a mental note. According to the measurements provided on the screen, the first object's length was just under thirty feet. He was about to circle and attempt to relocate whatever it was that caused the smear, when Grandma suggested, "Charlie, let's head in to shallow water." She motioned toward Freddy. He was visibly shaken by the whole eerie experience. "Let's go someplace where we can all see the bottom," Grandma persuaded.

Grandpa nodded and said, in his most official captain's voice, "To shallow water!"

"To shallow water!" Freddy echoed.

Grandpa pushed the throttle forward. "Full speed ahead!" he shouted over the engine's roar.

"Hooray!" the crew responded as they raced along, leaving the broad lake and its deep spooky water in their wake.

Chapter 6

That evening, instead of watching television with their grandparents, Bobby and Gina stayed upstairs. Bobby wrote in his notebook, describing the giant smear that had appeared on the boat's sonar. Gina sat at her table, drawing a picture of Champ and Little Champ swimming under *Crayfish* while everyone on board watched the tiny sonar screen. When she finished she showed Bobby.

"That's your best ever!" Bobby said, and he taped it to the dresser mirror.

Downstairs Grandpa sat staring at the television, but he wasn't paying attention to the show. All he could think about were the images he had watched all day on *Crayfish*'s sonar screen, especially the mysterious black smear. "That thing couldn't have been a log floating just off the bottom," he muttered.

"What?" Grandma asked. She was growing concerned about her husband. What had begun as a lighthearted adventure was becoming an obsession with him. "Charlie," she said pointedly, "I'll need you in the store tomorrow. It's getting busier every day. The tourists have arrived in full force."

Grandpa nodded but wasn't really listening. His mind was deep in the murky water of the lake.

"Charlie!" Grandma raised her voice. "Listen to me. You've been going out every day on the boat and I've had to do the work of two in the store. I'm tired of carrying the load and tired of this searching 'round for Champ!" She was about to say more when the doorbell rang, followed by hard knuckle knocking. "I'll get it," Grandpa said.

The knocking continued even as Grandpa was opening the door. It was Fred Sinclair, and he was not happy. "Charlie, what in the world have you been filling my son's head with?"

Grandpa stepped back and motioned for Mr. Sinclair to step inside.

"Freddy's scared to death! After supper I asked him to come with me and help me with my minnow traps, but he wouldn't even get in the boat. He says there's a monster in the lake! And that you saw it on your sonar screen."

Grandpa tried to explain, but Fred looked away and asked Grandma, "What's Charlie been saying to those kids? Freddy's home crying. He's afraid to go to bed—afraid he'll have a bad dream." He turned to Grandpa. "It's all your fault! All this nonsense about Champ!"

"I'm sorry, Fred," Grandpa said. He looked at Grandma. He saw her worried look. Fred Sinclair saw it too. He calmed himself and said, "I know you didn't mean to frighten Freddy. But this lake monster thing . . . I don't want you or Bobby and Gina telling him any more stories about monsters!"

"I know, Fred," Grandpa said. "I'm sorry." And he walked with him to the door.

After Fred had gone, Grandpa was upset. He put on a jacket and went outside to get some air.

Grandma noticed her grandchildren sitting on the stairs. They had been listening. "Don't worry, kids," Grandma told them. "Freddy's going to be fine. And so will Grandpa." She smiled warmly and whispered, "Go up and brush your teeth. I'm going out to talk to Grandpa. I'll be right back in to say good night."

Grandpa walked down to the marina and stood at the end of the dock. The lake was bathed in moonlight. He could see all the way across the water to the twinkling lights of cottages on the opposite shore, and beyond to distant mountain peaks. Yet when he looked down into the water near his dock, he could see nothing except blackness.

He heard footsteps behind him but he didn't turn

around. He knew it was Grandma. Soon he felt her soft touch on his arm. "I feel awful about little Freddy," he said, still looking out at the lake.

"I know," Grandma soothed. "But Fred's right."

"Of course he is," Grandpa replied. "It's just that we've seen men shot into space. We know what's on the moon. Yet we don't know what's at the bottom of this lake, less than four hundred feet down. We have no idea, really. And what's so discouraging is we don't even seem to care."

Grandma and Grandpa walked to where *Crayfish* was docked so they could sit together on the rail. "Listen, Charlie. It's not that we don't care. It's just a fact that people don't like to think about things unknown right in their backyards. It's frightening. It frightens me! Most folks prefer life's mysteries in safe, faraway places . . . places they can explore in daydreams without fear of any actual encounters . . . not in places where they live and work."

"You're right," Grandpa said. He laughed nervously. "I kinda let it get to me out there, didn't I? . . . Well, no more. No more searching. If I sail off again in the middle of the day, it'll be to take you and the kids to Sandy Point to swim. That's how it oughta be."

"Good." She took Grandpa's hand and pulled him

to his feet. "Now let's go inside. Our grandchildren are waiting for us."

Bobby and Gina were in their room at the window, watching their grandparents down on the dock. They couldn't hear the conversation. Both were thinking about Mr. Sinclair's angry visit. Suddenly Gina spoke. "Freddy thinks Champ is a monster. Monsters are scary." She looked at Bobby and asked, "Are you afraid of Champ?"

Bobby answered, "No. I'd like to see them both again—Champ and Little Champ—only I'd like Grandpa to be there so he could see them too."

Gina stared out at the moonlit lake and imagined Champ and Little Champ swimming side by side like two black swans in a silver sea.

"How about my good-night kisses?" Grandpa said, walking into the children's room with Grandma.

Gina ran and kissed her grandpa. Then she gave him a big hug. His cheeks felt cool and his collar smelled a little bit like gas from the boats at the dock.

Chapter 7

Grandpa kept his word to Grandma. For two weeks he didn't even mention Champ. And when a customer spoke of someone claiming to have seen Champ, Grandpa listened with interest, but refrained from telling stories about the fabled creature.

Then one busy afternoon, a young man came charging into the store, shouting, "Champ! We just saw Champ!" He dashed up to the counter and shouted right at Grandpa. "Film! I need film! Champ's still out there! Down in your marina!"

Everyone in the store rushed out to see, including Grandpa, Gina, Bobby, and Grandma.

Outside the marina dock was already crowded with curious villagers and motorists who had parked and left their cars to see what was going on. Even Freddy and his dad were there. When Fred Sinclair saw Grandpa coming, he yelled, "There's your Lake Champlain monster, Charlie! And look, it's brought a friend!"

Down in the shallow water, a pair of lake sturgeon wallowed in the soft silty bottom. The fish were huge, the largest more than five feet long. Everyone "oohed" and "ahhed." It was a marvelous sight.

"Those are sturgeon, folks," Fred Sinclair proclaimed. "Or as some people around here like to call them—Champ!" Laughing out loud, he turned and invited other passing motorists, "Come see Champ! It's Champ!"

Soon all the spectators were laughing. All except the Gennards and their grandchildren. Grandpa leaned down to Gina and Bobby and said softly, "That's not what you kids saw, is it?"

"No, Grandpa," they said.

"Come, Charlie, we must get back," Grandma said as people began to file off the dock. "There's no one minding the store."

On their way back, Bobby and Gina were stopped by Freddy and two older boys. Bobby recognized them as Freddy's cousin Tom and his friend Ed. Suddenly Freddy, who hadn't spoken to Bobby and Gina in the past two weeks, said, "So you both saw Champ, did ya?" The older boys laughed. "They saw Champ! Ha! Ha!"

Bobby tried to ignore the digs. He and Gina crossed the road.

But Freddy and the boys followed right behind,

teasing and taunting. Tom made a voice like a little girl. "Guess what, Grandpa? We saw a dinosaur in the lake!" The trio roared with laughter.

Gina spun around to face their tormentors. "There is so such a thing as Champ . . . And Little Champ too! We saw them! We saw them both!"

The boys were not impressed. They began to prance around, imitating Gina's voice. "We saw them! We saw them!" Freddy held two fingers against his head like horns. He rushed at Gina and mocked, "And Little Champ too . . . Yahoo!"

Bobby stepped in front of his sister. "You used to be our friend," he shouted at Freddy. "You're afraid of Champ!" He told Tom and Ed, "He's the one who thinks there are monsters in the lake, not us!" And with that he and Gina went up the steps and into the store.

Outside the three continued teasing, stomping around on the wooden porch, and chanting, "And Little Champ too . . . Yahoo!"

Inside the store Grandma and Grandpa were busy with customers. They didn't even notice their grandchildren come in. Bobby was angry. He ran ahead of Gina and went upstairs to their room. By the time Gina caught up with him, he had taken down her drawing of Champ and Little Champ and ripped it up. The pieces were all over the floor. "I wish we'd never told anyone what we saw!" he cried. "I wish we'd never seen Champ!"

Gina stooped and picked up the pieces of her drawing. She opened her dresser drawer and hid them under her socks.

Out in the lake in the deeper water just beyond the marina's outermost mooring, Champ and Little Champ swam slowly over the weeds. Using her snout as a shovel, Mother Champ uncovered a large bed of freshwater mussels. One by one she gobbled mussels down, shells and all, along with a few small pebbles here and there. They would add to the ballast of other pebbles and stones rolling around in her belly. It was this collection of stones that helped the creatures sink so quietly underwater without having to dive.

Little Champ was not interested in mussels. He swam around, poking his head here and there into the dense vegetation, looking for bluegills and perch. When he came upon a square mooring anchor and its chain, he stopped. He stretched his neck out and closely examined the cement block. He nipped cautiously at the rusty chain. Suddenly the chain, pulled by the boat it was attached to, swung around, loudly scraping its rusty links over the cement block, and Little Champ dashed away.

The next day was windy. All the boats moored in the marina tugged on their chains. Dark clouds were moving in from the west. Not many people came into the store, so Bobby and Gina could stay outside. They decided to fish off the dock. But once they had brought their tackle down to the marina, Bobby thought it would be more fun to fish from their grandfather's small rowboat. It was bobbing and rocking on the water, but tied securely to the dock.

Gina thought it felt just like being out on the lake. Bobby was baiting a hook when all of a sudden there was a great splash in the water. "What was that?" Bobby yelled in alarm. Then he heard laughing. Freddy, Tom, and Ed were back.

"Hey, look! Champ!" Ed yelled from shore. Tom threw another rock at the boat. It splashed in the water even closer to Bobby and Gina than the first.

"Stop that!" Gina shouted angrily.

Tom cupped his hands around his mouth and shouted back, "Don't you know you're supposed to go OUT in the boat to fish . . . not just sit in it tied to the dock?"

"Ha, ha, ha," the other boys laughed.

Bobby was so angry and embarrassed he couldn't speak. Instead he untied the dock lines and started the outboard motor.

"What are you doing, Bobby?" Gina yelled over the engine noise. "Grandma said we're supposed to stay near home!" She tried to climb out of the boat, but it had already moved too far from the dock.

Bobby ordered her, "Sit down, Gina! We're getting out of here! We're getting away from them!"

Gina sat back down. The water was choppy. She looked around in the boat. There were two old blue oars, an anchor and line, a bait bucket, and a couple of life jackets. She put one jacket on and threw the other to her brother. "Put it on!" she demanded.

But Bobby was too busy steering between the moored boats, heading the tiny boat out of the marina, away from the boys on shore.

As soon as Bobby had cleared the last mooring, he gunned the outboard and raced through the channel to the open lake. The wind grew stronger on the open water. Gina was getting scared. Just as she was about to yell for her brother to stop and head back, Bobby slowed down and shut off the engine. "STOP!" Gina blurted into the sudden silence.

"Don't worry, Gina," Bobby reassured her. "We'll fish here. See, we're really not that far from shore." He threw the anchor overboard and let out line until the anchor held. The boat bobbed quietly on the waves. Bobby put his life jacket on and helped Gina buckle hers more tightly.

"There. That's better," Bobby said. "Let's fish."

Chapter 8

After a while the wind died down and the lake calmed. But it was the kind of calm that often comes before a storm. Sky and water were uniformly gray. In the distance, thunder rumbled. "We'd better go back," Gina said. "Let's go back now, Bobby, while the lake is so still."

Bobby was watching Gina's bobber dip and dunk in the water. "You have a bite!" he whispered to Gina. "Get ready to reel in fast when I tell you to."

Gina gripped her rod tightly with her right hand and took hold of the reel handle with her left. She watched the bobber on the water—dip, dip, dunk.

"NOW!" Bobby yelled. "Reel it in!"

But before Gina made one turn of the reel handle, the boat rocked violently. She and Bobby threw down their fishing rods and dived for the safety of the floorboards. The boat rocked again. Then the bow rose a foot as if something was pushing it up from beneath.

"Whoa!" Bobby yelled. Gina wrapped her arms around the seat and held tightly. Abruptly the bow of the boat dropped down, hitting the water with a smack. Then all was still again.

Gina and Bobby stayed on the floorboards hugging each other, trembling, waiting for something else to happen. Nothing did. Together they crawled to the gunwale and peeked over the side. Down in the water they saw a small bass hooked and tugging on Gina's fishing line. The fish darted this way and that way, trying to break free. All at once the fish shot straight up, leaping out into the air. Something big rubbed against the bottom of the boat, and the bow rose up again.

Gina and Bobby clung to the gunwale as the boat tipped momentarily, then plopped back down into the water. Bobby glanced down in the lake and spotted the shape of an animal swimming away. "It's Champ!" he exclaimed.

Almost as if it had heard Bobby's voice, the creature swung slowly around and headed back toward the boat.

"No, it's Little Champ!" Gina said. She began to stand, but Bobby pulled her back down.

"Shhh!" Bobby whispered. "Keep down, so he doesn't see you."

Underwater, Little Champ slowly approached the hooked fish. So intent was he on the strange and erratic movements of the bass, he paid no attention to the floating boat, even when in passing beneath, his back rubbed up against it, slightly lifting the bow.

After circling the fish three times, Little Champ let himself sink and settle on the weedy lake bottom just eight feet below. Reaching up with his long neck, he continued to watch the fish as it frantically jerked about on the invisible line. Like a great snake being charmed out of a basket, Little Champ's head and neck swayed from side to side, his eyes fixed on the fish as it darted and tugged left and right.

Slowly Little Champ arched his neck. Quickly he struck out at the bass and missed. He opened his mouth and struck again. But because of the odd way the fish jerked around on the line, it was a difficult target, and Little Champ missed again. Just then he heard his mother's grunting call. In the next instant she was at his side, gently corralling him away from the fish and the boat.

Bobby and Gina were awestruck. They had seen it all up close. It was so real, yet unreal—Little Champ's neck swaying hypnotically in the water; his flat head and pointed snout; his two large protruding nostrils; his sharp white teeth and dark penetrating eyes. And

now they saw him and his massive mother swimming away.

Bobby hauled in the anchor. He then reeled in the bass, and put it in the bait bucket where it could stay alive and fresh. Then running the engine as quietly as he could, he caught up to and followed the creatures in the water.

Gina climbed up to the tip of the bow and kept her brother on course. Ahead she could see the two animals swimming just under the surface. The mother used her four huge flippers to paddle powerfully along. She looked much like an enormous sea turtle without any shell. Little Champ swam more like a seal, undulating his long neck and, at times, even corkscrewing through the water. Gina noticed as Little Champ spiraled along that his belly was much lighter in color than the rest of his body.

"Gina! Listen!" Bobby called forward. "Since Little Champ came after the bass once, he might come to it again. I've got a big hook Grandpa gave me. It's in my tackle box. We could use the anchor rope for a fishing line and the bass as bait."

Gina was astonished. "What are you thinking?" she questioned. "Did you see how big and strong even Little Champ is? And what do you think his momma would do? . . . Just wave good-bye?"

"But, Gina," Bobby argued, "think if we could hook the little one and gently tug and coax him back to shore, his mother might think he wanted to go with us and follow along. Then everyone would see Champ is for real."

Gina frowned at her brother. "You mean Freddy and his dumb cousin would see! Bobby, you're talking crazy." She climbed off her seat and reached for the bait bucket.

"No! Gina!" Bobby shouted too late as his sister spilled the bucket's contents, releasing the bass back into the lake.

"No way!" Gina said angrily. As she turned away from her brother, she spotted Champ and Little Champ surfacing side by side like a couple of porpoises. Then, in a wash of bubbles, they dived.

"They're gone!" Gina said, half disappointed and half relieved. "We should go home too."

Bobby slowed the boat to idle and looked out over the lake. Champ and Little Champ were nowhere in sight. Reluctantly he steered the boat around, heading it back to shore. As they turned, Gina and Bobby were both horrified to see how far they'd gone. The shore was miles away. They couldn't even tell where the marina was.

The sky blackened with storm clouds. The wind

was picking up again, blowing the small boat farther and farther away from the shore. Bobby raced the outboard and did his best to keep the bow of the boat pointed directly into the gusting wind.

Chapter 9

Back in the marina all the boats were pitching and rolling, pulling and straining their mooring lines. Sail lanyards rapped hard on their masts. Boats tied to the dock rocked wildly on choppy water. The wind blew stronger with each gust, and large heavy raindrops began to fall.

Grandpa ran out onto the store's porch just as a streak of lightning sizzled near. *CRRAACK—BOOM!* The sound followed.

"Bobby! Gina!" Grandpa yelled. "Bobby! Gina! Where are you kids? Come inside!"

Freddy and the other boys came running by, and Grandpa asked, "Freddy! Have you seen Gina and Bobby?"

Freddy skidded to a stop on the rain-slicked road. "Yes, Mr. Gennard! They were going out in your rowboat to fish." Rain poured down. Freddy shielded his head with his arm and ran home.

Inside the store the lights dimmed as another bolt of lightning cracked in the sky over the island. Grandma went to the door, hoping to see Grandpa bringing the children. But she saw only Grandpa coming back from the marina. He was soaking wet. "Freddy says Gina and Bobby are out on the lake. They've taken the rowboat."

"Are you sure?" Grandma asked.

"Yes, I checked the dock. The rowboat's gone." Grandpa went inside and got his yellow slicker. "I'm going out on *Crayfish* to find them," he said. His voice was shaking, partly from being wet and cold and partly from fear.

"Oh my!" Grandma worried. She knew how Grandpa hated boating in foul weather. "I'll go too!" she insisted.

But Grandpa said, "No! You have to stay here. Keep the CB turned on. If anything happens, I'll call and you can get help out to us fast."

Bobby and Gina were still far out on the lake. The rain had not yet reached them, but the wind had gotten worse. Again and again it blew the bow of the little boat off course. Bobby yelled to Gina, "Pile all our gear in the center of the boat, and get down there yourself!" She did, and the shift of weight to the center of the boat made it easier for Bobby to keep the boat pointed into the wind.

The little engine strained as it pushed the boat up and over the oncoming waves. Then, without warning, the engine died. "What's wrong?" Gina asked. Bobby unscrewed the fuel cap and looked into the tiny gas tank. It was empty.

With no power to push it, the boat drifted freely, slowly turning one side to the wind. A wave smashed the boat lengthwise. "Grab the oars!" Bobby shouted. "If we don't turn the boat back around into the wind, we could go over!"

Gina reached for an oar. Another wave hit the boat broadside. Gina and Bobby struggled to row. A gust of wind carrying lake water sprayed them. Then the rain came.

Bobby and Gina rowed and rowed until the boat's bow was again pointing into the wind. But that was all they could do. The wind was too strong, the waves too high. "We're not getting anywhere!" Gina cried as she rowed.

"I know!" Bobby shouted. "But we've got to keep rowing so we don't spill!" Bobby turned his cap around so it wouldn't blow away. A bolt of lightning cracked in the darkening sky.

Gina rowed even harder. She was crying out loud.

So was Bobby. Together they managed to keep the boat windward.

Grandpa charged along at full throttle, surfing *Crayfish* over the waves. His eyes repeatedly scanned the water ahead, searching for a dot or a shape that could be a small boat. When he was one mile from shore, it occurred to him that no matter where his grandchildren had been, the storm would have blown them north, then east. With the wind at his stern, he ran with the storm.

About two and a half miles out, Grandpa spotted the rowboat. It was still way off. Through the binoculars he saw Bobby and Gina in the center of the boat, rowing like mad. Grandpa raced *Crayfish* onward, signaling them with the horn.

"TOOT-TOOT!" Gina heard the horn first. She twisted around in her seat and looked over the bow.

"TOOT-TOOT!" *Crayfish*'s horn sounded again.

"It's Grandpa!" Gina shouted. "He's coming to get us!"

Gina let go of her oar and waved her arms in the pouring rain. Bobby stopped rowing also. The boat veered in the wind and another large wave socked it hard, knocking both of them down onto the floorboards.

"TOOT-TOOT!" Grandpa signaled again. He waved to the children hunkered down in the little boat. The rowboat bobbed wildly, up and down, its blue oars dangling from their oarlocks.

With his grandchildren only a hundred yards away, Grandpa raced on. *Crayfish*'s deep bow sliced full-speed through the water. Then suddenly the whole boat ground to a sickening halt. Immediately Grandpa realized what he had done. He looked over the rail. "The shoal!" he said, smacking his forehead with the palm of his hand. "I forgot all about it."

Bobby and Gina wondered what was going on. "Grandpa! Grandpa!" they called as they drifted farther away.

Grandpa climbed forward shouted, "Sit up and row! You have to row to me! I can't go any farther!"

Bobby and Gina sat on the center seat and rowed as hard as they could. The rain was beginning to let up and the wind seemed to be dying down. But there was still enough chop in the waves to make it hard going.

Grandpa stood on *Crayfish*'s bow and coached them along. "That's it! You're coming!" When they veered off course, he corrected, "More to your side, Bobby," or "a little more to Gina's side." Finally they had rowed close enough for Grandpa to reach down and grasp the bow of their boat. He guided the rowboat along *Crayfish*'s rail to a strong cleat near the stern, and with a few quick wraps of braided line, the boat was secured.

Grandpa helped Gina onto *Crayfish*'s deck, then reached a hand to pull Bobby aboard. The three of them hugged and held each other. Their ordeal was over. "Wait until I tell your dad and mom how you both handled those oars!" he said proudly. Grandpa hugged Bobby and Gina again. The storm clouds had moved on, pushing and shoving their way east over the mainland. The sun came out. The lake calmed.

Crayfish's engine was still idling. Grandpa went to the console. "You kids stay close to me, and hold on." He eased the engine into forward and gradually pushed the throttle to full. The engine roared but the boat did not budge. Grandpa throttled down, eased into reverse, and raced the engine again. *Crayfish* still did not go. That was it. Grandpa quit trying and shut the engine off. He left the CB on.

Bobby and Gina and their grandfather looked down over the side and into the water. They could see the shoal they were on. "Geesh!" Grandpa winced. "We're really stuck!" He leaned way over the side to look under the boat. "Lucky thing, though. It looks like we're on a sandy spot. This shoal is mostly rocks."

Bobby jumped down into the rowboat and handed the oars up to his grandfather. "Let's try pushing off with these," he suggested. But after trying only a minute or so to pole *Crayfish* off the ridge, Grandpa knew it was useless. He sat down on the deck to rest.

"Charlie . . . Charlie . . . are you there? Over." Grandma's voice came over the CB. "Charlie . . . are you all right? Have you found them? Over."

Grandpa rose to his feet, picked up the hand mike, and gave it to Gina.

"Hi, Grandma!" Gina said.

Grandma was jubilant. She called back, "Thank God! Oh, Gina. Bobby. You had us so worried!"

Bobby spoke into the mike, "I'm sorry, Grandma. It was all my fault. Gina told me not to . . ."

"It's all right, Bobby," his grandmother interrupted. "Now you tell your grandfather to hurry home!"

Grandpa took the mike. "Adele!" he began sheepishly. "It's Charlie. We have a problem. Over."

Grandma called back. "What? What's wrong?"

Grandpa leaned back against the console and tipped his cap back on his head. Finally he said, "We're stuck on the shoal."

"The shoal!" Adele called. "Charlie, you know that shoal like the back of your hand!"

"I know. It was stupid of me. But with the storm

61

and the waves, I wasn't thinking of anything but getting to the kids' boat."

The CB crackled a few seconds. Then Grandma's voice suddenly coming through louder and clearer, said, "Yes, Charlie, I can imagine how it must have been." There was another pause, followed by the sound of Grandma's laughing. "And I can just picture you now, Charlie Gennard, pouting over your baby being stuck like a lump on that shoal."

Gina and Bobby laughed with her. Grandpa smiled. Then his face straightened. "We're gonna need help to get off, Adele." He looked at the mike as he spoke. "Are you sure you know where we are? Over."

Grandma called back, still chuckling, "Charlie, everybody on the island knows where the shoal is!"

Gina tried not to laugh.

"Oh, yeah, right," Grandpa said, growing more and more embarrassed. Then he transmitted, "See if you can find someone to come out and pull us off."

"Okay, Charlie. You just stay put." Grandma giggled. "Over."

Chapter 10

Gina was bursting to tell her grandfather the reason they had gone so far out on the lake. She whispered to her brother, "What about Champ?"

Bobby was not eager to tell. He pulled Gina closer and whispered, "If we tell Grandpa, it'll just get him started again. Grandma will worry. People will make fun."

"Look, kids! Look at all the mayflies!" Grandpa called. "The storm must have triggered a mayfly hatch."

The air over the water was snowy with thousands of cream-colored flies. Grandpa reached out and a fluttering fly alighted on the back of his hand. He moved his hand slowly toward him and held the mayfly so Gina and Bobby could see it up close. He spoke softly. "For most of its life a mayfly is wingless and lives underwater. Then one day when it reaches maturity, it swims to the surface, sheds its old skin, and emerges winged and ready to fly."

Bobby and Gina looked closely at the tiny fly. Finally it flexed its wings and flew away.

It was a marvelous sight, all the flies in the air, scores more still floating on the water. Soon fish began rising to the surface to feed. Perch and bass gulped down floating flies. Some fish leaped clear out of the water after flies in the air.

In the midst of the flies and fish an enormous black hump emerged momentarily, then quickly sunk. "What was that?" Grandpa asked loudly.

Gina shouted, "It's Champ! Grandpa, it's Champ!"

The hump rose again and lingered on the surface while the water all around it spattered and splashed with fish fleeing the scene. The hump rose a little higher, revealing three smaller lumps on its spine. Then directly in front of the hump, the long neck of the mother lifted gracefully until it stood six feet up out of the lake. Water dripped from her snout. Her mouth held three wriggling perch. Mayflies fluttered all around her head and landed in numbers on her wet skin.

Grandpa was awestruck. Gina whispered to him, "It's the momma."

Grandpa looked down at his granddaughter. Then back to Champ. Tears filled his eyes. "It's absolutely marvelous!" he said softly.

Bobby nudged his grandpa. "Look! Under the water near Champ—that's Little Champ!"

Grandpa squinted to see through the glare on the lake surface, but he could make out only the light-colored oval of Little Champ's belly underwater.

The mother lowered her neck even more slowly than she had raised it. When it was nearly parallel to the water, she dipped down and sank out of sight. But she did not go away. They watched her path underwater by the successive groups of terrified fish leaping on the lake surface. When she had cruised to within twenty feet of the boat, she momentarily surfaced again, porpoising up through a great concentration of floating mayflies. Grandpa could see her front flippers paddling. Her strokes were so powerful, they sent shock waves through the water, rocking *Crayfish's* hull.

Farther out two more large humps suddenly surfaced. "There's more!" Gina said, keeping her voice low and trying to contain a sudden rush of excitement. The distant humps separately rose and fell in the water. Grandpa thought he saw the head of one of the animals poking up. But neither raised a long neck out of the water. After only three or four seconds, both humps submerged.

Gina looked all around for Little Champ and finally

spotted him underwater just beyond the tethered rowboat. He was snorkeling by with only his two protruding nostrils sticking up out of the water. "Look, Grandpa! Up close! Little Champ!" Gina whispered excitedly. But by the time Grandpa and Bobby looked, Little Champ had sunk out of sight.

Bobby climbed up and stood on the rail. He looked down in the water but saw no sign of either Champ or Little Champ.

Grandpa peered into the water. "I see something!" he said, pointing down. "Yes, I think it's Little Champ."

Gina wanted her grandfather to see Little Champ as closely as she and Bobby had. She spotted the chain of plastic fish still lying in the corner of *Crayfish's* deck. Quickly she broke off a bright yellow fish and then hopped down into the rowboat.

"Gina, get back up here!" Grandpa said.

"Watch, Grandpa!" Gina said confidently. Ducking down behind the gunwale so Little Champ wouldn't be able to see her, Gina tied the plastic fish to the end of her fishing line and lowered it over the side.

Grandpa and Bobby stayed back away from the rail so they wouldn't be seen but where they could look down into the water between the two boats. Gina jerked the plastic fish up and down so it moved just like the bass she had hooked. After a minute or so, a long shadowy shape appeared below the line.

"It's working!" Bobby whispered.

Grandpa saw the shape moving closer, and quietly exclaimed, "Sure enough, Gina. Here it comes!"

Little Champ rose steadily to the lure and gently bumped it with his snout. "Well, I'll be!" Grandpa said under his breath. Gina was delighted. She pumped her rod harder, making the plastic fish move more wildly in the water. Excited by the lure's movements, Little Champ swirled around in a circle, churning the water with great force, which pushed against the boats.

Grandpa felt *Crayfish* slide ever so slightly on the shoal. It gave him an idea. "Keep it up, Gina!" he said, walking slowly backward to the console.

Little Champ rushed around the lure again, creating another powerful swirl. *Crayfish* rocked to one side and slid a bit more. Little Champ playfully circled the bright yellow lure, this time so excitedly his thick tail thumped *Crayfish*'s hull. The boat started sliding again. Grandpa turned the ignition key and jammed the engine into reverse. "Hold on, kids!" Grandpa cautioned as the boat, still sliding, began backing off the shoal under power. The sudden commotion spooked Little Champ and he swam quickly away.

With one final sand-grinding slide, *Crayfish* was

clear of the shoal and floating freely again. Everyone cheered, "Whoopie! Hooray!" Grandpa spun the wheel and steered away from the hazardous shoal. Bobby helped Gina climb up from the rowboat and back onto *Crayfish*'s deck.

Before heading for shore, Grandpa, Gina, and Bobby looked back toward the shoal just in time to see two dark humped backs, one large and one smaller, emerge in a wash of white foam. They watched the two humps, hoping for a last sight of the long graceful necks arching up out of the water. But none showed. Then side by side the humps silently submerged and the lake surface was calm again. Gina said softly, "Good-bye."

On their way home they met Mr. Sinclair's boat coming to their rescue. Freddy was in the boat near his dad.

Mr. Sinclair slowed down to idle and sat scratching the back of his head. Grandpa eased *Crayfish* close. On the deck behind Freddy he saw a neat coil of strong towing rope. "Thanks for coming to get us, Fred," Grandpa said, smiling. "I appreciate it."

"How the heck did you get off the shoal, Charlie? Adele said you were really stuck!"

"We were," Grandpa replied. He looked at Bobby

and Gina and winked. Then he turned back to Fred. "We had some unexpected help. We got a good nudge from a big ol' musky!" Gina and Bobby laughed. Fred and Freddy laughed at the joke too, but they had no idea what it meant.

Grandpa, still chuckling, pushed *Crayfish* clear of the Sinclairs' boat. Mr. Sinclair spun around and raced back toward the island. Grandpa slipped *Crayfish* in gear and putted slowly behind.

Bobby looked at his grandfather and said slyly, "A big ol' musky gave us a nudge." They all laughed again.

Gina turned serious. She asked, "Why didn't you tell them what we saw, Grandpa? . . . Why didn't you tell them what really helped push us off?"

Grandpa looked at Gina, then back to the water ahead. He thought for what seemed a long while and finally answered, "Some folks believe only what they see with their own eyes, and even then sometimes they don't believe. Nothing you say can change that." He looked down at Gina and continued, "Then, there's folks who can't help but believe—in mystery, in the infinite possibilities of life."

"That's us!" Bobby said, and he shouted out, "Here's to mystery!"

Grandpa cheered. "Here's to Champ!"

"And Little Champ too . . . Yahoo!" Gina added.

Grandpa sounded *Crayfish*'s horn. *"TOOT-TOOT!"* The marina lay just ahead.

Miles from the Gennards' marina, miles from any shore, down deep where the water is always cold and dark, Champ and Little Champ were on their way to another part of the vast lake. They were in no hurry. They had all the time in the world.

AUTHOR'S NOTE
COULD CHAMP EXIST?

Lake Champlain is a great and wondrous place. Eighty-three known species of freshwater fish inhabit its waters. There is also a rich variety of aquatic and semiaquatic reptiles, amphibians, mammals, and birds.

For many years, along with the sightings of known animals, people have reported much rarer sightings of something large and unknown living in the lake. Over the years this unknown has been called the Lake Champlain Sea Serpent, then the Lake Champlain Monster, and now simply "Champ." Since the mysterious sightings go back hundreds of years, those who have studied the Champ phenomena have logically concluded that, if Champ does exist, not one but a small breeding colony of Champ animals would have to be living in the lake. (This same conclusion has been reached at Scotland's Loch Ness regarding "Nessie.")

The Champ animals people report seeing do not

appear threatening. Quite the contrary, they seem shy and gentle like manatees or whales. But eyewitness accounts do not describe whales or manatees or even large seals. Remarkably most eyewitnesses describe a creature closely resembling a plesiosaur—a large aquatic reptile long thought to be extinct. But how could a cold-blooded reptile survive the frigid waters and winters of Lake Champlain? Some scientists have suggested that plesiosaurs may have been warm-blooded or developed a certain degree of warm-bloodedness.

Whatever the Champ phenomena are eventually discovered to be, if they are indeed animals, they are already protected from harm or harrassment by laws in New York and Vermont, the two states that share most of Lake Champlain.

As a naturalist with a particular interest in aquatic life, I have wondered how such creatures would live and how they could go mostly undetected living so close to people. Slowly the story of *Little Champ* developed in my mind.

For the past seven years I have spent a good deal of time boating, fishing, and photographing water-fowl on Lake Champlain. I have never seen Champ. I hope to someday.

ABOUT THE PUBLISHER

Onion River Press reissues books by Vermont authors and illustrators. It is our belief that many wonderful titles have been allowed to lapse by publishers who lack a connection to our Vermont community or a commitment to Vermont authors. We work closely with our authors, resulting in a unique collaborative effort and great books. Our authors are integral to our process of keeping Vermont books alive. We want all generations past, present and future to enjoy these literary treasures.

Onion River Press
We bring books back to life.

www.onionriverpress.com